The Adventures
of
Danika and Dalilah

To the moon with Casey June

ISBN 979-8-89043-500-2 (paperback)
ISBN 979-8-89043-501-9 (digital)

Christian Faith Publishing
832 Park Avenue
Meadville, PA 16335
www.christianfaithpublishing.com

Printed in the United States of America

The Adventures of Danika and Dalilah

to THE MOON with CASEY JUNE

DIONNE CARPENTER

ILLUSTRATED BY: TIMOTHY LAMBERT

Danika and Dalilah are identical twins who have Down syndrome. Both of the girls have hearing loss and use sign as another way of communication.

Danika and Dalilah loved to look at the moon and stars. One night, the girls asked their sister Casey June to take them to the moon. Casey June loved the moon too! She agreed to take them to the moon very soon. She thought long and hard about how to do this. The girls were so excited and could hardly contain their excitement.

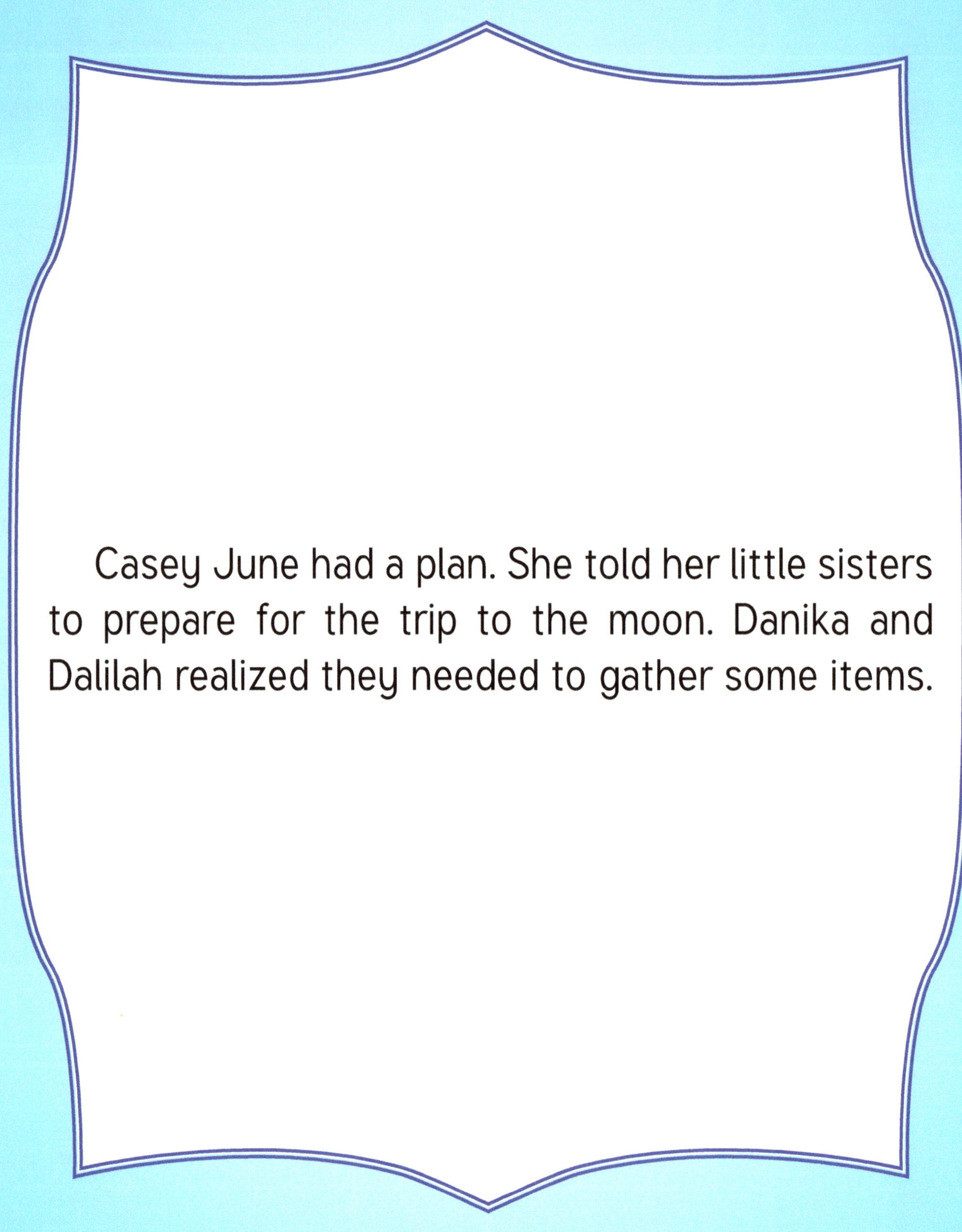

Casey June had a plan. She told her little sisters to prepare for the trip to the moon. Danika and Dalilah realized they needed to gather some items.

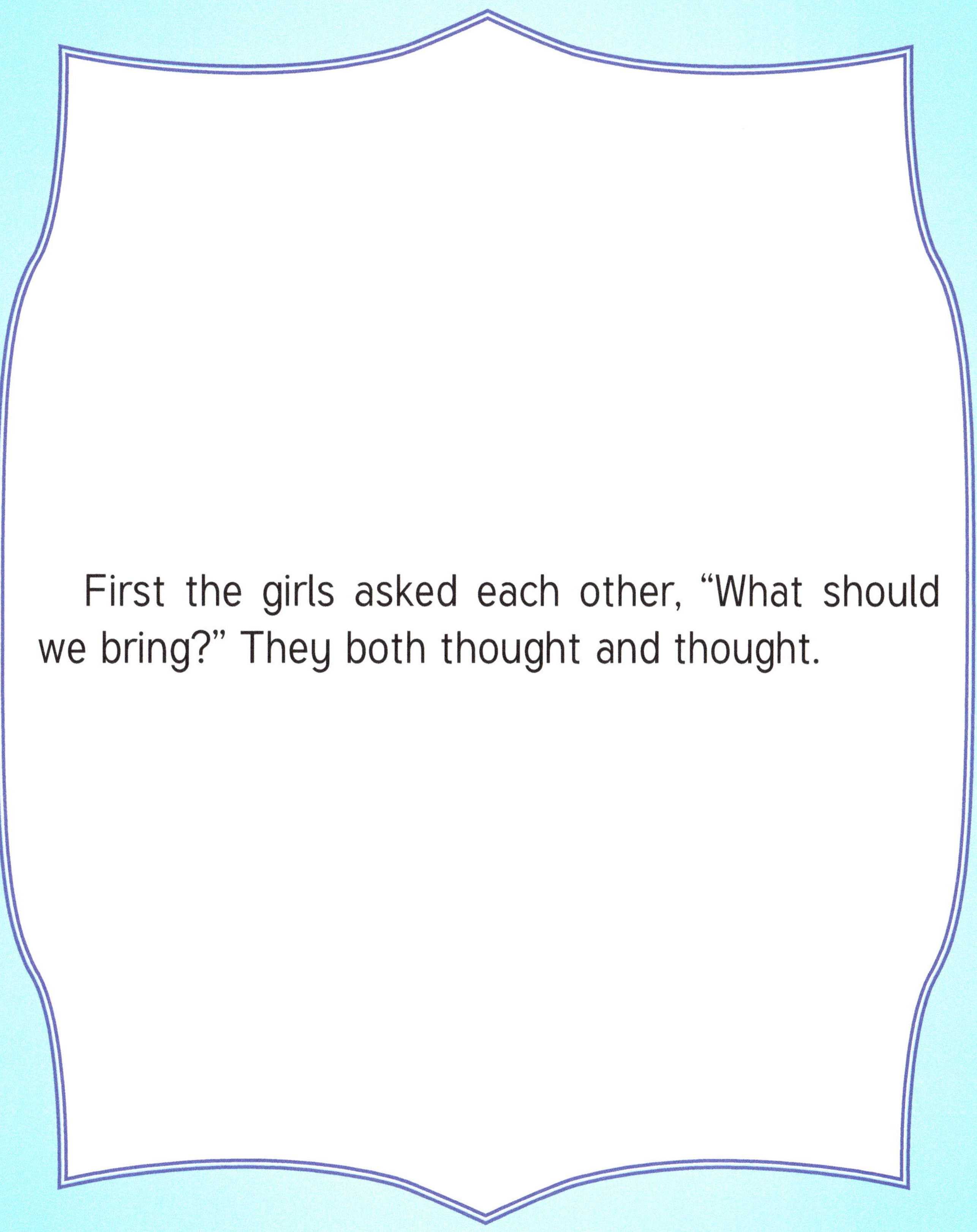

First the girls asked each other, "What should we bring?" They both thought and thought.

COOK
CHIPS
SNACKS
DANIKA
AND
DALILAH

Dalilah said, "I think we need to bring a backpack." Danika said, "Good idea." So both girls began to add items to the bag. They put in a few water bottles, a camera, and, of course, snacks for their adventure to the moon. Danika reminded Dalilah to bring their headsets, as loud noises bother them.

All three sisters were super excited about seeing the moon. Months before this, they would go to their aunt Kelly's land to look at the moon and stars through a big telescope. Casey would bring her telescope every Saturday night to the empty field. They sat for hours observing the moon and stars.

The telescope is so clear they could see all of the craters on the moon. When they looked at all the stars shining, they were reminded of something.

They said, "Look, Casey June, WE SHINE LIKE THE STARS!"

About the Author

Casey June

Dionne lives in central New York with her children. She is the mom of five and three of whom are young adults. The twins' girls came as a surprise to her in 2014. The girl's Down syndrome was not known at the time of birth.

She is an elementary teacher, so she has read numerous children's books over the years of teaching. One day while at work, she had a thought about what it would be like to write her own children's book, books about her daughter to help change the world. She felt like she was given a special gift from God when it came to Danika and Dalilah having Down syndrome. Dionne knew she needed to share with the world the beauty that has been given to her and her family. Every day is truly an adventure with Danika and Dalilah. She is counting on everyone to go on these exciting and fun loving journeys. Some of these adventures will consist of fiction and nonfiction. The girls and Dionne are planning their next adventure and story soon.